THE CASE OF THE CHOCOLATE CHIP COOKIES

One day Sherluck Bones visited the Kennelwood Cookie Factory. The owner showed him the big safe with the burglar alarm where the secret chocolate chip cookie recipe was locked up. Then she introduced him to Marvin Mastiff, the new night watchman.

"Say," Marvin said, "last night I had a dream that the burglar alarm was broken. I suggest you have it checked."

After Marvin left, Bones said, "I think you should look for a new night watchman. Marvin is a very bad one."

Do you know why Bones said that? Turn to page 16 to see if you're right!

The Sherluck Bones Mystery-Detective Book 1

Jim Razzi

Pictures by Ted Enik

Mystery Writers of America Presents
New York Lincoln Shanghai

The Sherluck Bones Mystery-Detective Book 1

All Rights Reserved © 1981, 2003 by Jim Razzi

No part of this book may be reproduced or transmitted in any form or by any means, graphic, electronic, or mechanical, including photocopying, recording, taping, or by any information storage retrieval system, without the written permission of the publisher.

Mystery Writers of America Presents
an imprint of iUniverse, Inc.

For information address:
iUniverse
2021 Pine Lake Road, Suite 100
Lincoln, NE 68512
www.iuniverse.com

Originally published by BANTAM Books, Inc.

Cover art copyright © 1981 by Bantam Books, Inc.
Illustrations copyright © 1981, 1983 by Bantam Books, Inc.

ISBN: 0-595-29088-4

Printed in the United States of America

Contents

Introduction	6
Bones at the Cookie Factory	7
Mixup at the Airport	17
The Crooked Cowboy	25
Who Gets the Prize?	35
Scotson Solves a Case	43
The Whistling Crook	53

Introduction

Sherluck Bones, the world-famous detective, lives in Kennelwood, U.S.A. His good friend Scotson lives there, too. Together they have solved many mysteries, crimes, and puzzling events around town. No clue escapes the eagle eye of Bones. No puzzle is too hard for his quick brain to solve.

See if you're as good a detective as Bones is. In each story in this book there is a mystery, crime, or puzzle to solve. There is always a clue for you, so pay attention and try to come up with the solution along with Bones and Scotson. .

Bones at the Cookie Factory

The Kennelwood cookie factory was famous for its chocolate chip cookies. Everyone in Kennelwood loved them.

ABthe owner of the factory, Sally Spitz, was a good friend of Sherluck. One day Bones and Scotson decided to pay her a visit. Sally met them at the gate and took them for a tour of the factory. They walked past big vats full of hot melted chocolate. There were mounds of

cookie dough on tables and many busy cookie cutting machines. Scotson was getting hungry as he watched the cookies being made. Then Sally took them to the bakery where the cookies were baked. Bones was very interested in everything.

"I understand that the recipe for your chocolate chip cookies is a secret," he said to Sally.

"Yes," she answered. "We keep the recipe in a big safe that has a burglar alarm."

"I say," said Scotson, "I'm sure no thief would ever be able to steal *that* recipe."

"Yes," Sally answered, "and as a double protection, we have a night watchman. He is here from seven o'clock in the evening until nine o'clock in the morning."

"An alert fellow, I suppose?" asked Bones.

Sally said that she thought so but didn't know for sure, since he was new. She went on

to explain that her regular night watchman was on vacation. A fellow named Marvin Mastiff had been hired to take his place. Last night had been his first time on the job. Bones nodded.

Since it was about nine in the morning, they happened to meet Marvin coming from work. He was a big, slow-moving fellow. Sally stopped to talk to him.

"Well, Marvin," she said, "how did you get on with your first night on the job?"

"Fine," he said. "I had no trouble at all."

Sally turned to Bones to say something, when Marvin interrupted.

"Say, I almost forgot," Marvin said. "Last night I had a dream that the burglar alarm was broken. My dreams usually come true." Marvin puffed out his chest and tried to look important. "So I suggest that you have the alarm checked."

Sally looked surprised and said that she would do that right away. Marvin just nodded and went off saying, "Well, I'd better go home and get some rest, I want to be alert again tonight."

Sally smiled and turned to Bones. "Well, I'm impressed with Marvin," she said. "He certainly looks as if he knows what he's doing. I'm going to check that alarm right now."

"Before you do that," said Bones, "why don't you look for a new night watchman?"

Scotson and Sally opened their mouths in surprise.

"Why do you say that?" sputtered Sally.

"Because Marvin is a very bad night watchman," answered Bones.

"But how can you know that, Bones?" asked Scotson. "You hardly know the fellow."

"I know enough to know that he should be fired," answered Bones. He then went on to explain why.

Do you know why Marvin was a bad night watchman?

The solution is on the next page.

SOLUTION TO
Bones at the Cookie Factory

Marvin said that he had a "dream" that the alarm was broken. If he was dreaming, he must have been asleep on the job. Bones realized that fact right away and told Sally.

Mixup at the Airport

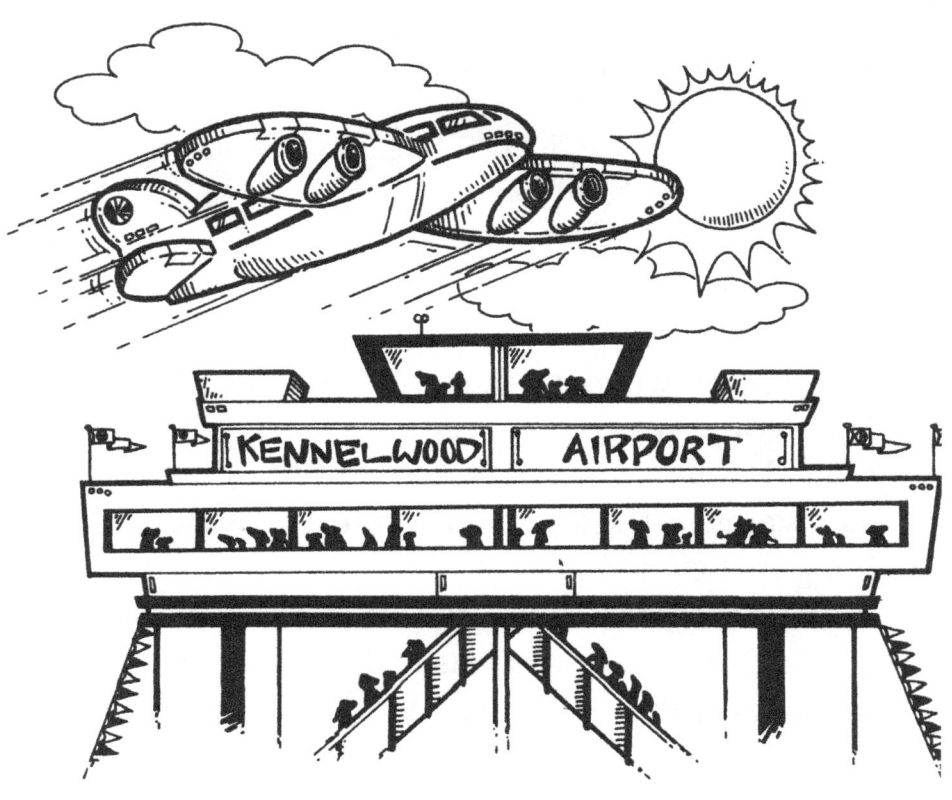

The Kennelwood airport was a busy place. Everyone was hurrying off somewhere, loaded down with bags and suitcases. Scotson watched the scene with interest as Bones bought their tickets.

They were off for a vacation on a warm tropical island. Bones was looking forward to lots of swimming. Scotson was going to lie in the sun. Just the thought of it made him feel warm all over.

Suddenly a lot of yelling at one of the airline ticket counters snapped Scotson out of his daydreaming. He and Bones looked over and saw Willy Whippet and Gary Greyhound having an argument. Bones got their tickets and the two friends went over to see what the problem was. When the airline clerk saw Bones, he sighed with relief.

"Sherluck Bones! Thank goodness," he said. "Maybe you can solve this problem."

Bones and Scotson asked what the argument was about and the clerk told them. It seemed that Willy and Gary had exactly the same kind of suitcase. Gary said that Willy had picked up his suitcase by mistake and had opened it up. He also said that now Willy was claiming that the suitcase was his.

"Why would he do that?" asked Bones.

"Because I have lots of new things in it and Willy wants them!" shouted Gary.

"That's a lie!" Willy shouted back. "This *is* my suitcase!"

Bones ignored Willy for the moment and asked Gary what was in his suitcase.

"Well," answered Gary, "I have new summer clothes, a new bathing suit, and a new underwater camera."

"Hmmm," said Bones. "Well, before we go any further, let's open up the other suitcase and see what's in it."

They opened up the other suitcase and saw that it was full of well-worn winter clothes.

"Ha," said Willy with a smirk, "what a bunch of dull stuff. I'm glad that's not *my* suitcase."

"It is too your suitcase!" shouted Gary. "And you have mine!"

"I do not!" Willy yelled back. "And furthermore I have to catch my plane." He waved his ticket in the air.

Gary pulled out his ticket also and yelled, "I have to catch my plane too. So give me back my suitcase!"

Scotson looked from one to the other, as if he were watching a Ping-Pong game.

"By heavens, Bones," he said, "what a mix-up! How can we ever solve this problem?"

"Oh, I think that will be easy enough to do, Scotson," said Bones. Then he asked Willy and Gary to show him their tickets.

What does Bones hope to find out?

The solution is on the next page.

SOLUTION TO
Mixup at the Airport

Bones simply wanted to know where Gary and Willy were going. He knew that one of them would have a ticket for a place that was cold because of the winter clothes in one suitcase. He also knew that one of them would have a ticket for a place that was warm because of the summer clothes, bathing suit, and underwater camera.

As it turned out, Willy was lying. He had a ticket to a place up north, where it was snowing. But Gary had a ticket for the same warm island that Bones and Scotson were going to.

The Crooked Cowboy

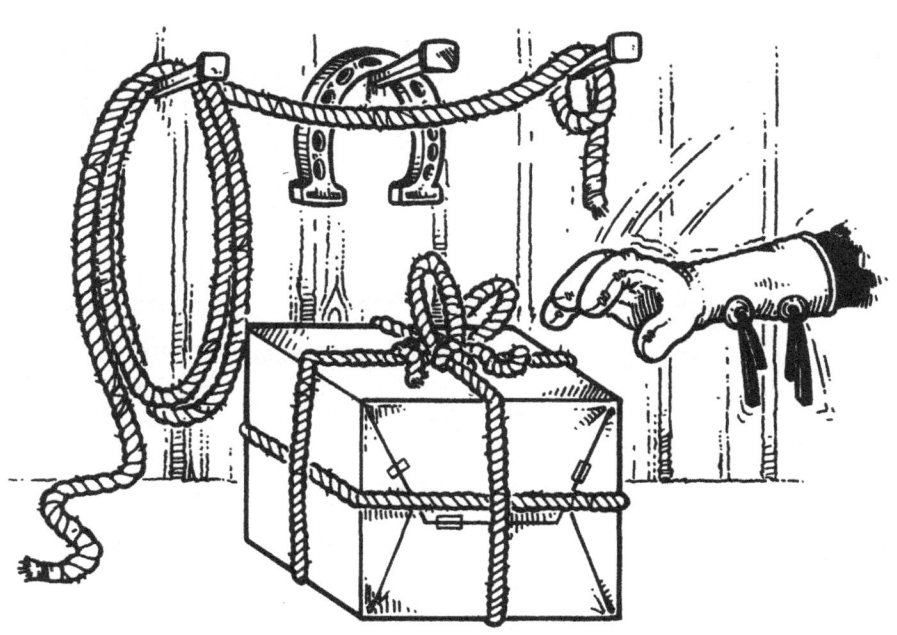

Bones and Scotson were at the Kennelwood Dude Ranch for a day of horseback riding. Scotson wasn't very happy about the idea, since he was a little afraid of horses. But he put on a brave face and hoped for the best.

Tommy Terrier, the owner of the ranch, greeted them at the stables with three horses. Tommy was an old friend and was going out riding with them. When Scotson saw the horses, he said, "Er, which one is mine?"

"Old Thunder here," said Tommy, patting the back of a big spotted horse.

"Th-thunder?" stammered Scotson.

"Don't worry," laughed Tommy, "you'll be fine."

"Who, who's worried?" answered Scotson as he carefully got on his horse. Bones and Tommy got on their horses, and the three rode off.

After a while, Scotson became more sure of himself. He started to puff out his chest.

"I guess not *everyone* can ride Thunder, eh, Tommy?" he asked proudly.

"Well, that's true," answered Tommy. "We usually save him for youngsters and beginners."

"Oh, I see," said Scotson, turning red and clearing his throat.

Bones turned his head and tried not to laugh. Just then, Tommy looked at his watch.

"I think I had better be going back," he said. "There is a big rodeo parade tonight and someone sent me a new cowboy hat to wear. I don't know what color it is because I haven't opened the package yet. I want to see if it will go with the rest of my cowboy costume."

Bones and Scotson said that they didn't mind returning, so the three riders headed home. When they got back to the ranch, they were met by Waldo Whippet, the ranch foreman. He had a worried look on his face.

"Someone's been in the ranch house and stolen that gift package you received today, boss!" he blurted out.

"Who was the lowdown coyote who did it?" asked Tommy angrily.

Waldo said that he didn't know yet. But it had to be one of the three cowboys who worked on the ranch. They were the only ones who were in and out of the ranch house all day. He went on to say that he hadn't said anything to them yet.

"Hmm," said Bones. "Let's go see what we can find out."

They found the three cowboys, Freddie Foxhound, Danny Doberman, and Charlie Cocker, near the bunkhouse. Bones started to

question them. First he asked Freddie, "Do you know anything about a package with a hat in it that was stolen from the ranch house?"

Freddie looked blank and said, "Of course not. What am I supposed to know? I didn't take any package. That's all I know."

Bones said, "Hmm." And then he asked Danny, "Do you know anything about this hat theft at the ranch house?"

Danny looked sulky and answered, "Of course I don't. What do I look like, a hat thief?"

Bones said, "Hmm," again. Then he turned to Charlie. "What do you know about this stolen hat?" he asked.

Charlie looked hurt and said, "Why ask me? What would I know about a stolen hat? Anyway, I don't need a white hat. I have plenty of them."

Bones just nodded and then turned to Tommy and Waldo.

"Well," said Tommy, "since they all deny it, how can we ever find out which one is the thief?"

"Oh, that's easy," answered Bones. "As a matter of fact, I can tell you who the thief is right now."

"Who is it?" asked Tommy with a surprised look.

Who is the thief and how did Bones know?

The solution is on the next page.

SOLUTION TO
The Crooked Cowboy

Charlie is the thief. When Bones questioned him, Charlie said, "Anyway, I don't need a *white* hat."

Bones remembered that Tommy had said that he didn't even know the color of his new hat yet. He then realized that only the thief (who would have opened the package) would know what color it was.

Who Gets the Prize?

Sherluck Bones and Scotson were attending an award dinner at the Kennelwood Mountain Climbers Club. A prize was being given to Sammy Sheepdog. He was being honored for becoming the first member to climb to the top of Eagle Mountain alone. No one had actually seen Sammy at the top. He had climbed the mountain *alone*. But Sammy was known for never telling a lie, so everyone took his word for it.

The president of the club was just about to give Sammy his prize. Then Louie Labrador burst into the room. Louie was a club member who was jealous of Sammy. He was always trying to make Sammy look bad.

"That prize belongs to me!" shouted Louie. "Sammy Sheepdog is lying!"

All the members opened their mouths in surprise. Scotson turned to Bones. "I say, Bones, what an unusual event," he said.

"It is indeed, Scotson," answered Bones. "Let's see what this is all about."

They went over to Louie, who by this time had a small crowd around him. Everyone was talking at once. When they saw Bones, they quieted down. Bones spoke directly to Louie.

"What makes you think that *you* deserve the prize?" asked Bones.

"Because," said Louie with a smirk, "I climbed to the top of Eagle Mountain, alone, myself. But I can prove it. Sammy can't!"

Bones then asked Louie to show them his proof. Louie gave a smug smile and pulled

out an instant photo. "I had to pick this up at home," he said. "That's why I was late."

Everyone pressed forward to peer at the photograph. It was a picture of Louie standing alone on the flat top of Eagle Mountain. There was no one else in sight.

Scotson sighed and said, "Well, Bones, this tops it all. The photograph certainly proves that Louie is telling the truth. I guess the prize will have to go to him."

"Not so fast, Scotson," said Bones. "I think this photograph proves that Louie is lying!"

"What do you mean?" stammered Scotson.

Do you know why the photograph proves that Louie is lying?

The solution is on the next page.

SOLUTION TO
Who Gets the Prize?

When Bones saw the photograph, he knew that Louie was lying when he said that he had climbed to the top alone. He knew that there had to be someone else with Louie. The someone who took the instant photo!

When caught in his lie, Louie admitted that Danny Dalmatian helped him climb to the top. And he was the one who took the photo.

The prize was then given to Sammy.

Scotson Solves a Case

Bones and Scotson were visiting Sir Lonny Labrador, a famous art expert. Sir Lonny was showing them his art collection. Bones painted for a hobby himself, so he knew quite a lot about art. Scotson, on the other hand, knew next to nothing.

"Here's a genuine Picatto," said Sir Lonny, holding up a strange looking picture.

Scotson said, "Ah yes, very good indeed!"

Sir Lonny looked again at the painting. Suddenly he said, "Oops! It's upside down."

Scotson gave a little cough and said, "Ah, yes. A picture of a clown at the circus."

Bones just smiled and asked Lonny if he could take a closer look.

While Bones and Lonny were studying the picture, Scotson strolled over to the wall to look at some other paintings. He spied a picture of a flower scene. Scotson loved flowers, so he looked more closely. While doing this, he brushed against another picture nearby. It was a painting of a Dutch windmill. Some wet paint from the picture rubbed off on his sleeve. "Drat it all!" he said to himself. He was embarrassed by his clumsiness, so he didn't say anything to the others.

Sir Lonny and Bones were just finishing their talk, when Scotson came back.

"Yes, Bones," Sir Lonny was saying, "I'm happy to say that I'm an expert on art."

Bones just nodded.

Then Sir Lonny asked Bones and Scotson to stay for tea. After a pleasant hour spent eating cookies and talking about art, it was time to leave. Suddenly Sir Lonny said, "Oh, I almost forgot. I must show you my newest find. It's a genuine painting by a famous artist who lived a long time ago." Sir Lonny went to the wall and took off the picture of the Dutch windmill.

"I haven't paid for this yet," he continued. "It is being sold by a new art dealer in town. I will pay him tomorrow."

Bones and Scotson looked at the painting. "Yes, it's very good," said Bones. "A real masterpiece. What do you say, Scotson?"

Scotson looked at the picture for a little while and suddenly said, "By George, that painting is a fake! Don't pay a red cent for it!"

Sir Lonny and Bones looked at Scotson in amazement. "How do you know that?" they both asked.

How did *Scotson* know that the painting was a fake?

The solution is on the next page.

SOLUTION TO
Scotson Solves a Case

Sir Lonny had said that the picture was painted by a famous artist who lived *a long time ago*. Therefore the painting of the Dutch windmill should certainly have been *dry!* Scotson knew from his accident that it wasn't. Therefore, he figured, the painting was a fake that had only been painted recently.

The Whistling Crook

Bernard Beagle, the violinist, called Sherluck Bones and Scotson to his home. Bernard was a well-known musician around town, but Bones didn't think much of his playing. In any case, it seemed that someone had stolen one of Bernard's violins during the night. It was very valuable, and Bernard was very upset about losing it.

"Tell us what happened," said Bones.

"To start with," said Bernard, "I'm sure it's that whistling crook who stole it."

Bones nodded. He and Scotson knew that there had been a lot of robberies in Kennel-

wood lately. In each case, the victim had heard someone whistling in the night. Then, the next day, the victim discovered that something had been stolen from his house.

"Why do you suspect the whistling crook?" asked Scotson.

"Well," answered Bernard, "I went to bed early last night because I was tired."

Scotson and Bones nodded.

"About one o'clock in the morning," Bernard continued, "someone passed by my window whistling a tune."

Bones and Scotson nodded again.

"Then, a few minutes later, the same person must have knocked over my garbage can, because I heard an awful racket. I woke up and fell out of bed!"

"You poor fellow!" cried Scotson.

"Yes," said Bernard. "Well, after that, I looked out the window and saw my garbage can tipped over. I couldn't see anyone around, so I went back to sleep. But when I awoke this morning, I discovered that my violin was gone!"

"Is it insured?" asked Bones.

"Oh, yes," Bernard answered. "If it's

stolen, I get a lot of money from the insurance company. But that's not important. I want my violin back, not the money!"

"Of course you do, old boy," murmured Scotson. "But don't worry. Bones and I will catch this whistling crook and get your violin back in no time at all."

Bones looked at Bernard sternly and said, "I don't think we have to catch the whistling crook to get Bernard's violin back, Scotson. I think Bernard already has his violin. It was never stolen. He just wants to get money for nothing!"

"How dare you!" Bernard shouted.

"How can you say that, Bones?" asked Scotson in surprise.

"Because the story that Bernard told us has a big mistake in it," answered Bones.

What did Bones mean?

The solution is on the next page.

SOLUTION TO
The Whistling Crook

Bernard told them that someone had passed by whistling a tune at one o'clock in the morning. Then he said, "the same person must have knocked over my garbage can, because I heard an awful racket. I *woke up* and fell out of bed!"

If he woke up *then*, he must have been sleeping when the whistling person passed by. But if he was sleeping, how could he know that someone passed by whistling?

When Bones pointed this out, Bernard confessed that he had made up the whole story. He had pretended that the violin was stolen so he could collect the insurance money. This way he would have the money *and* the violin.

ABOUT THE AUTHOR

JAMES RAZZI is the bestselling author of numerous game, puzzle, and story books, including the Slimy's Book of Puzzles and Games series. Well over two and a half million copies of his books have been sold in the United States, Britain, and Canada. One, *The Star Trek Puzzle Manual,* was on the New York Times bestseller list for a number of weeks. His fascinating book *Don't Open This Box!* was picked as one of the "Books of the Year" by the Child Study Association.

ABOUT THE ILLUSTRATOR

TED ENIK is a playwright, a set designer, a magazine artist, and a cartoonist as well as a children's book illustrator. He is the illustrator of *Bob Fulton's Terrific Time Machine* by Jerome Beatty, Jr. and the Slimy's Book of Puzzles and Games series, which were written by Jim and Mary Razzi, all published by Bantam Books. Mr. Enik lives in New York City.

0-595-29088-4

Made in the USA
Coppell, TX
28 October 2021